# MULTIPLYING & DIVIDING PUZZLES

Karen Bryant-Mole

Illustrated by Graham Round

Edited by Robyn Gee

Series editor: Jenny Tyler

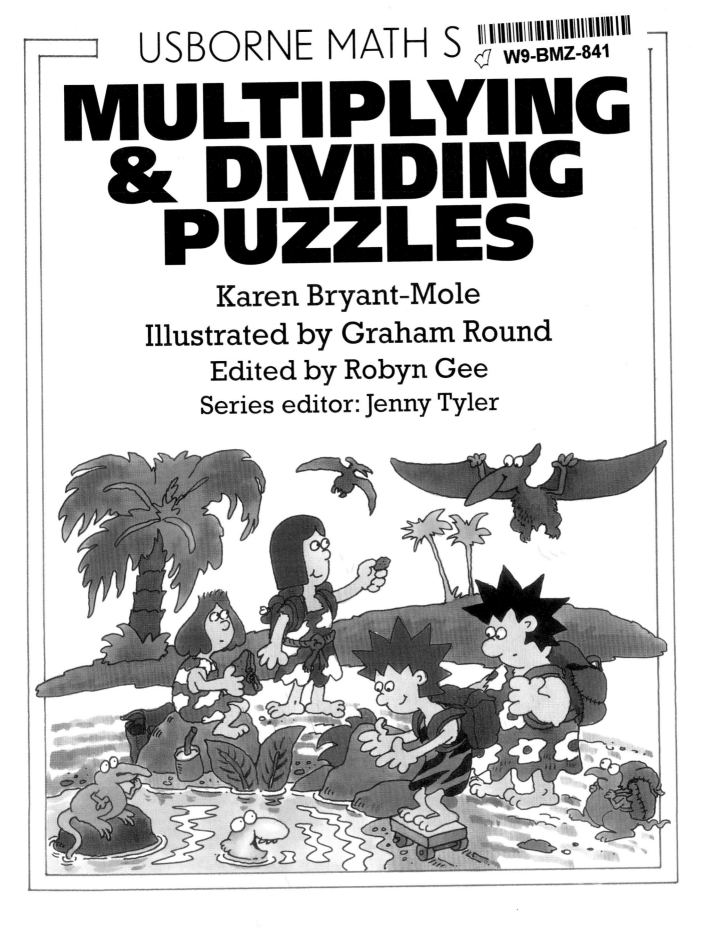

# What is multiplication ?

Imagine you wanted to find out how many legs there were altogether on these 8 dinosaurs. You could write a problem like this:

$$4 + 4 + 4 + 4 + 4 + 4 + 4 + 4 = 32$$

This is a bit long though. You could think of multiplying 4 legs by 8 instead. You can write this as:

$$4 \times 8 = 32$$

You can only use multiplication when there are the same number of things in each group. You couldn't write a multiplication problem about the number of legs on two dinosaurs and a pterodactyl for instance, because the dinosaurs have 4 legs, but the pterodactyl really only has 2.

You would have to write an addition problem like this:

$$4 + 4 + 2 = 10$$

There are two questions below. One can be answered by writing an addition problem and the other by writing a multiplication problem. Write either + or x after the questions below to show which is which.

If there are 9 cups and 3 have 1 straw, 3 have 2 straws and 3 have 3 straws, how many straws are there altogether ?

If there are 7 children coming and they each want 2 cakes, how many cakes must be baked ?

# Multiplying and dividing

In this book you will find division problems as well as multiplication problems. Division and multiplication are very closely linked. If you want to divide 28 by 7 it helps if you know that 7 multiplied by 4 is 28.

Division problems are about sharing amounts into equal groups. If 4 children had 12 rock cakes to share between them, they would each get 3 cakes. The problem for this would be:

$$12 \div 4 = 3$$

Can you draw a ring around the multiplication problem that helps you solve the division problem below ?

$$20 \div 4 =$$

$$2 \times 4 = 8$$

or

$$3 \times 4 = 12$$

or

$$4 \times 5 = 20$$

You can find the answers to all the puzzles in this book on pages 28 to 32.

Try not to use a calculator for any of the puzzles in this book.

Can you figure out whether you would use a multiplication problem or a division problem to answer the questions below? Write either x or ÷ in the boxes.

*If there are 5 rows of stones in a wall and 15 stones in each row, how many stones are there altogether ?*

*This mammoth eats the same amount of food each day. If he eats 112 pounds in a week, how much does he eat each day ?*

# Meet the Og family

### Grandma Og

Grandma Og enjoys flower arranging. When she counts she likes to count in twos.

### Grandpa Og

Grandpa Og is a stickball fan. He likes to count in fives.

### Mrs. Og

Mrs. Og breeds dinosaurs. They usually have 3 babies at a time, so she likes to count in threes.

### Mr. Og

Mr. Og goes for long walks. He counts in sixes as he walks.

### Mog Og

Mog Og is good at skipping. While she skips she counts in tens.

### Zog Og

Zog Og likes playing discus with his friends. He is very good at counting in fours.

Name: _____
18, 24, 30, 36, 42 ___
___ ___

Name: _____
9, 12, 15, 18, 21 ___
___ ___

Name: _____
6, 8, 10, 12, 14 ___
___ ___

Can you figure out which stone belongs to which member of the Og family? Put the correct name at the top of each stone and then write the next three numbers in each sequence.

Name: _____
25, 30, 35, 40, 45 ___
___ ___

Name: _____
30, 40, 50, 60, 70 ___
___ ___

Name: _____
8, 12, 16, 20, 24 ___
___ ___

5

# The market

Mrs. Og is at the market. Two of the traders are arguing about a box of apples. They want to know how many apples there are in the box. One man says that the problem is 4 x 6. The other man says it is 6 x 4.

Mrs. Og explains that they are both right. One man is counting the rows across and multiplying them by the number of columns. The other man is counting the columns and then multiplying them by the number of rows.

The important thing is that it doesn't matter, because 4 x 6 and 6 x 4 both give the answer 24.

Can you write two problems for each of the boxes of fruit below ?

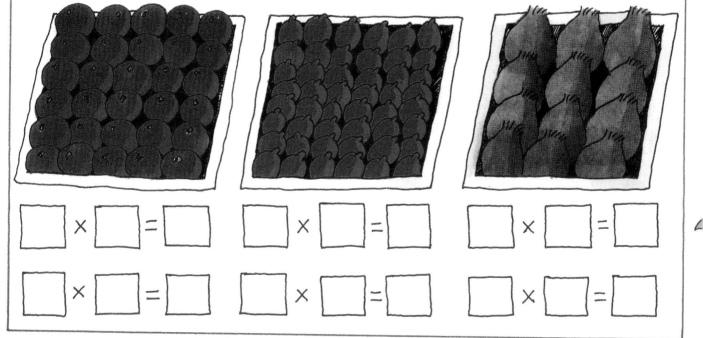

$\square \times \square = \square$    $\square \times \square = \square$    $\square \times \square = \square$

$\square \times \square = \square$    $\square \times \square = \square$    $\square \times \square = \square$

The people of Ogtown use pebbles as money.

One of the traders has decided to make himself a chart to help him figure out the cost of his customers' shopping.

When he filled in the cost of 3 items at 7 pebbles per item, he drew his finger across from 3 until he got to the square that was

underneath 7. He knew that 3 x 7 was 21, so he wrote 21 in that square.

Can you fill in the rest of the missing numbers for him?

An item is anything that the trader sells, like an orange or a pineapple or a banana.

You will only actually need to figure out the problems in the shaded area. The rest, like the problems on the opposite page, use the same numbers in a different order.

If you need to, you can use this chart to help you do some of the other problems in the book.

Cost per item in pebbles

Number of Items

7

# Perilous Pond

Grandpa Og and Zog have been playing with their discus near Perilous Pond. Unfortunately Grandpa threw the discus into the pond.

There are lots of stepping stones in Perilous Pond but not all of them are safe. If Grandpa or Zog step on a wobbly one they will fall in. This would be disastrous, because there are fierce, hungry, prehistoric fish in the pond, waiting to eat them.

Near the pond is a block of stone. It provides a key to which stones are safe. Can you help Zog and Grandpa find a safe route to their discus ? You need to figure out the answers to the problems and draw a ring around the numbers on the safe stones.

# The circus

The Ogs are at the circus, watching the jugglers. The juggler in blue has the number 8 on his suit. He is juggling with four balls which show the numbers 1, 2, 4 and 8. These numbers are called the factors of 8.

Can you figure out the factors of the other numbers on the jugglers' suits and write them on the balls? Each juggler is juggling with the correct number of balls.

The factors of a number are all the numbers that can be multiplied by another number to give you that number.

The factors of 8 are 1, 2, 4 and 8, because you can make 8 by multiplying 1 by 8, 2 by 4, 4 by 2 and 8 by 1.

Common factors are numbers that appear in more than one factor list.

The factors of 4 are 1, 2 and 4. The factors of 6 are 1, 2, 3 and 6. So, 1 and 2 are common factors of 4 and 6.

See if you can help Mog and Zog find the common factors of these pairs of numbers.

10 and 8 ☐ ☐

18 and 12 ☐ ☐ ☐ ☐

8 and 20 ☐ ☐ ☐

10 and 15 ☐ ☐

Can you write the factors of each seat number on the back of the seat?

12

10

20

6   7

13   14

19   20

11

# The secret code

Mog and Zog are pretending to be spies. Mog has written a message to Zog, using their secret code. Below you can see what the message looks like.

| 78 | 64 | 72 | 87 | 72 |
|----|----|----|----|----|
|    |    |    |    |    |

| 42 | 86 |
|----|----|
|    |    |

| 42 | 80 | 96 | 42 | 86 | 42 | 85 | 84 | 72 |
|----|----|----|----|----|----|----|----|----|
|    |    |    |    |    |    |    |    |    |

| 42 | 80 | 48 |
|----|----|----|
|    |    |    |

| 42 | 80 |
|----|----|
|    |    |

| 78 | 64 | 72 |
|----|----|----|
|    |    |    |

| 99 | 42 | 80 | 48 |
|----|----|----|----|
|    |    |    |    |

| 85 | 90 | 78 | 78 | 84 | 72 |
|----|----|----|----|----|----|
|    |    |    |    |    |    |

To find out what Mog is telling Zog you have to crack the code.

Each letter of the alphabet is represented by a number. To find out what the number is you have to complete the multiplication problems. Zog has already figured out what A is, can you help him with the rest ?

A
23
× 4
——
92
——

B
17
× 5
——

——

C
44
× 2
——

——

D
14
× 7
——

——

J
15
× 4
——

——

K
16
× 3
——

——

L
14
× 6
——

——

M
31
× 3
——

——

Always multiply the units first.

S
43
× 2
——

——

T
13
× 6
——

——

U
15
× 5
——

——

Zog is asking Mog a question in code. Can you figure out what it is ?

| 56 | 64 | 72 | 87 | 72 |

| 42 | 86 |

| 93 | 75 |

| 88 | 92 | 99 |

Can you write the answer in code too ?

E
36
×2
___

___

F
13
×7
___

___

G
18
×3
___

___

H
16
×4
___

___

I
14
×3
___

___

N
20
×4
___

___

O
15
×6
___

___

P
11
×9
___

___

Q
13
×5
___

___

R
29
×3
___

___

V
12
×8
___

___

W
14
×4
___

___

X
19
×5
___

___

Y
15
×5
___

___

Z
17
×3
___

___

If you have any tens to carry over, write them under the bottom line of the problem. Don't forget to add them on, after you have multiplied the tens.

13

# The Ogtown picnic

Every year the people of Ogtown get together for an enormous town picnic. This year the Ogs have volunteered to do the shopping. They don't know exactly how many people will be coming, but they have estimated that they will need to cater for 1000 adults, 100 children and 10 dogs.

Can you calculate how many of each item they will have to buy and fill in the shopping list?

2 drinks per child

8 cans of dog food per dog

5 ice creams per child

**Ogtown Picnic Shopping List**

bones
cans of drink
little cakes
buns
hot dogs
chocolate drops
packs of peanuts
strawberries
sandwiches
cans of dog food
slices of cake
cartons of mango juice
ice creams

# At the beach

Mog and Zog are spending the day on the beach with their friends, Mig and Tig Ig. They are building sandcastles. They have collected lots of shells, pebbles and pieces of seaweed to decorate them. They want to share the shells, pebbles and seaweed equally between them.

Count the number of shells. Can you figure out how many each child will get?

Decorate each castle with the correct number of shells.

Can you do the same with the pebbles and the seaweed?

The fishermen want to divide their catch equally between them. Can you help them by counting up the number of fish in the basket and then drawing the correct number of fish on the trays next to the fishermen?

All the fishermen should have an equal number of fish.

# Off to Igville

Mr. Og is an avid walker and Mrs. Og sometimes likes to join him for a day out walking in the hills around Ogtown.

Today they are going to walk from Ogtown to Igville. Mr. Og wants to go one way, but Mrs. Og wants to go another way. They decide to go different ways and see who gets there first.

## How to play

To find out who arrives first, put a counter or coin on Mr. Og's starting point and one on Mrs. Og's. Look at the problem on Mr. Og's space and figure out the answer. There should be a remainder. Move forward the same number of spaces as the remainder. Do the same with the problem on Mrs. Og's space. Now go back to the space where Mr. Og's counter is and do that problem. Continue to take it in turns to do a problem on each path. Who gets there first?

START

$24 \div 5$

$48 \div 9$

$37 \div 7$

START

$7 \div 4$

$23 \div 4$

$25 \div 6$

In the problem $14 \div 3$, 3 will go into 14 more than 4 times, but not as much as 5 times. So the answer is 4 remainder 2, because 4 threes are 12 and the difference between 12 and 14 is 2.

When you divide a number by another number it does not always divide equally. Sometimes there is a number left over. That number is called a remainder.

$44 \div 5$

$75 \div 9$

# Shopping

Grandma and Grandpa Og have just returned from their local supermarket, Dinomart.

Here is the receipt, showing what they bought and how much they paid. Can you figure out the cost of each individual item and fill in the prices on the labels?

| Dinomart | pebbles |
|---|---|
| 6 loaves of bread | 150 |
| 8 apples | 40 |
| 3 boxes of butter | 66 |
| 5 cakes | 175 |
| 4 cans of soup | 68 |
| 2 cauliflowers | 46 |
| 5 pizzas | 315 |
| 3 boxes of cereal | 96 |
| 1 jar of jam | 27 |
| 9 sausages | 81 |
| 8 bananas | 48 |
| 7 yogurts | 56 |
| 3 bags of potatoes | 87 |
| 9 carrots | 36 |
| 8 bottles of milk | 128 |
| 4 blocks of cheese | 96 |
| TOTAL | 1515 |

Thankyou for shopping at Dinomart

To find out the price of a single item, divide the total cost by the number of items.

To divide a large number, such as 224, by a small number, like 7, write it down like this:

$$7\overline{)224}$$

You can think of 224 as 22 tens and 4. First ask yourself how many 7s there are in 22 tens. There are 3 tens remainder 1 ten. Write it like this:

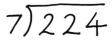

The remainder 1 is actually 10. So you have 10 + 4 left, which is 14. There are two 7s in 14, so write 2 above it.

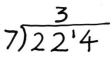

So 224 ÷ 7 = 32

Not all of this shopping is for the Og family. Grandma and Grandpa have an elderly friend called Mrs. Ug. She finds walking difficult and so Grandma and Grandpa do her shopping for her.

Here is Mrs. Ug's shopping list. Can you figure out how much she owes Grandma and Grandpa?

| Mrs. Ug's shopping | Pebbles |
|---|---|
| 3 bottles of milk | |
| 4 carrots | |
| 2 cakes | |
| 1 box of cereal | |
| 2 blocks of cheese | |
| 3 sausages | |
| 2 yogurts | |
| 1 pizza | |
| 4 apples | |
| 2 loaves of bread | |
| 1 box of butter | |
| 3 bananas | |
| TOTAL | |

pebbles
pebbles
pebbles
pebbles
pebbles
pebbles
pebbles
Pebbles
Pebbles
pebbles
pebbles
pebbles
pebbles
Pebbles
pebbles
pebbles
pebbles

milk
yogurt
soup
Jam
butter

21

# Stickball

Stickball is a very popular game in Ogtown. It is easy to play. There are two sticks 15 paces apart. A batter stands by one stick and a bowler stands by the other stick. The bowler throws the ball and the batter hits it as hard as possible. The batter has to run between the sticks as many times as possible before the ball is thrown back to the bowler. Each time the batter touches a stick it counts as one run.

The Ogs and the Igs belong to a stickball team called the Pterodactyls. So far this season they have played six matches.

On the right you can see the number of runs that Mr. Og has scored in each match. You can use these scores to figure out the average number of runs that Mr. Og scored in each match.

| Match | 1 | 2 | 3 | 4 | 5 | 6 |
|---|---|---|---|---|---|---|
| Mr. Og's runs | 23 | 46 | 13 | 56 | 39 | 63 |

To figure out an average you have to add together all the numbers and then divide the answer by the amount of groups of numbers.

In Mr. Og's case the total number of runs is:

$23+46+13+56+39+63=240$

Divide this by the number of matches:

$240 \div 6 = 40$

| Average |
|---|
| 40 |

Can you figure out the average scores for the rest of the team ?

| Match | 1 | 2 | 3 | 4 | 5 | 6 | Average |
|-------|----|----|----|----|----|----|---------|
| Mrs. Og | 46 | 30 | 42 | 38 | 20 | 46 | |
| Zog | 58 | 24 | 67 | 14 | 5 | 48 | |
| Mrs. Ig | 21 | 47 | 38 | 26 | 11 | 55 | |
| Mr. Ig | 32 | 26 | 54 | 31 | 17 | 38 | |
| Tig | 63 | 22 | 36 | 11 | 16 | 62 | |

Grandma and Grandpa Og watch all the Pterodactyl's matches. Grandpa loves calculating averages. He doesn't just figure out each player's average number of runs, he figures out lots of other averages as well. Here are the figures he has written down in his notebook. Can you figure out all the averages ?

| | Total number of Pterodactyl runs | Total number of opposition runs | Number of Spectators | Number of sandwiches eaten |
|---------|------|------|------|------|
| Match 1 | 243 | 180 | 62 | 36 |
| Match 2 | 195 | 240 | 73 | 24 |
| Match 3 | 250 | 182 | 54 | 34 |
| Match 4 | 176 | 165 | 88 | 38 |
| Match 5 | 108 | 295 | 65 | 43 |
| Match 6 | 312 | 234 | 120 | 29 |
| Average | | | | |

# Mrs. Ig's flower shop

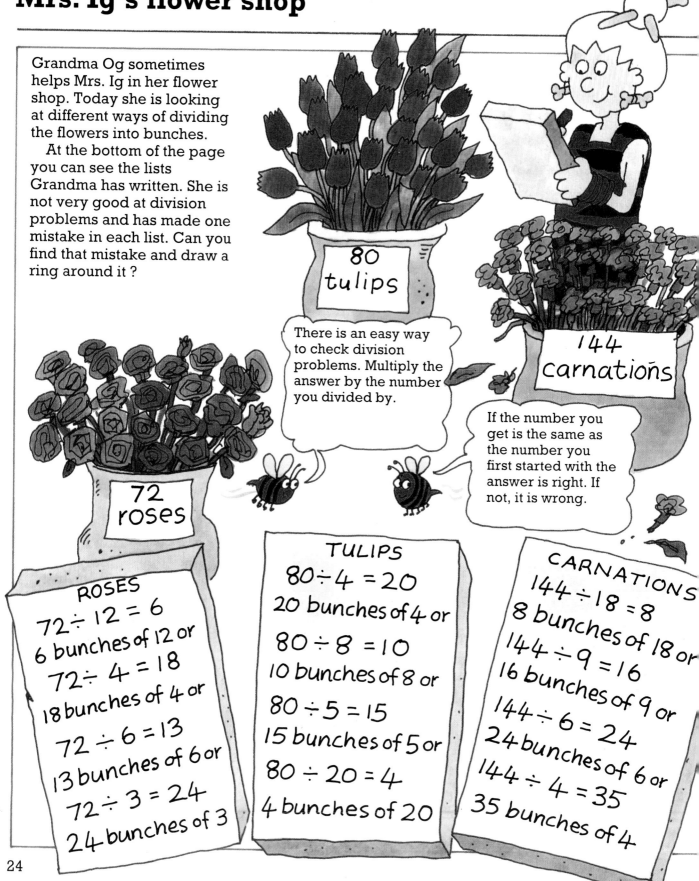

Grandma Og sometimes helps Mrs. Ig in her flower shop. Today she is looking at different ways of dividing the flowers into bunches.

At the bottom of the page you can see the lists Grandma has written. She is not very good at division problems and has made one mistake in each list. Can you find that mistake and draw a ring around it?

**80 tulips**

**144 carnations**

There is an easy way to check division problems. Multiply the answer by the number you divided by.

If the number you get is the same as the number you first started with the answer is right. If not, it is wrong.

**72 roses**

ROSES
72 ÷ 12 = 6
6 bunches of 12 or
72 ÷ 4 = 18
18 bunches of 4 or
72 ÷ 6 = 13
13 bunches of 6 or
72 ÷ 3 = 24
24 bunches of 3

TULIPS
80 ÷ 4 = 20
20 bunches of 4 or
80 ÷ 8 = 10
10 bunches of 8 or
80 ÷ 5 = 15
15 bunches of 5 or
80 ÷ 20 = 4
4 bunches of 20

CARNATIONS
144 ÷ 18 = 8
8 bunches of 18 or
144 ÷ 9 = 16
16 bunches of 9 or
144 ÷ 6 = 24
24 bunches of 6 or
144 ÷ 4 = 35
35 bunches of 4

Mrs. Ig is checking yesterday's takings. There were 411 pebbles in the cash register and she has a list of how many bunches of flowers she sold and what price they were.

| | Pebbles |
|---|---|
| 6 bunches at 8 pebbles a bunch | 48 |
| 3 bunches at 13 pebbles a bunch | 39 |
| 8 bunches at 9 pebbles a bunch | 72 |
| 14 bunches at 6 pebbles a bunch | 84 |
| 4 bunches at 21 pebbles a bunch | 86 |
| 12 bunches at 7 pebbles a bunch | 84 |
| TOTAL | 413 |

When she has finished multiplying and adding up the answers, she ends up with a different number to the actual number of pebbles in the cash register.

Can you spot her mistake and draw a ring around it?

You can check a multiplication problem by dividing the answer by the number you multiplied by. The number you get should be the same as the first number in the multiplication problem.

# Speedy Sid's tips

Mog and Zog's cousin, Sid, has come to stay. Sid is brilliant at multiplication. He is so quick that his friends call him Speedy Sid.

Sid has some secret ways of remembering some of his tables. He decides to let Mog and Zog in on his secrets. Here are Speedy Sid's terrific tips.

To multiply by 11 write the other number twice.

If you are multiplying by 10, just write the other number and then a 0.

To multiply by 9, hold your hands up with your palms toward you. Call each finger a number from 1 to 10.

If you want to multiply 8 by 9, put down finger number 8. You should have 7 fingers to the left of 8 and 2 to the right.

To multiply by 5, hold up the same number of fingers as the other number and count them in 5s.

The number of fingers to the left tells you the number of tens and the number to the right tells you the number of units. So 8 x 9 is 7 tens and 2 units, or 72.

If you are multiplying even numbers by 6, write the number that is half the other number and then the other number.

Sid is testing Mog to see how fast she can do her multiplication problems using his terrific tips.

Mog takes 3 minutes to do these problems. Can you beat Mog's time? When you have finished, check your answers and add on 10 seconds for every wrong answer.

Don't forget, you can change the order of the numbers in a multiplication problem and still get the same answer. So if you know a terrific tip for either of the numbers in the problem, use it.

$3 \times 5 =$

$10 \times 6 =$

$9 \times 4 =$

$8 \times 11 =$

$9 \times 9 =$

$3 \times 10 =$

$11 \times 9 =$

$5 \times 5 =$

$8 \times 6 =$

$3 \times 9 =$

$9 \times 10 =$

$5 \times 8 =$

$9 \times 2 =$

$11 \times 6 =$

$2 \times 5 =$

$5 \times 7 =$

$9 \times 8 =$

$6 \times 9 =$

$10 \times 7 =$

$4 \times 5 =$

Sid has made up a number puzzle for Zog. Can you help him fill it in?

Across
1  $6 \times 6$
3  $5 \times 4$
4  $6 \times 5$
6  $3 \times 11$
7  $9 \times 5$
8  $5 \times 9$
9  $7 \times 10$
10  $9 \times 6$
12  $10 \times 2$
13  $2 \times 11$

Down
2  $7 \times 9$
3  $9 \times 3$
5  $7 \times 11$
6  $7 \times 5$
7  $4 \times 10$
8  $11 \times 4$
9  $8 \times 9$
10  $10 \times 5$
11  $2 \times 6$

27

# Answers

## Pages 2 and 3

### What is multiplication?

Imagine you wanted to find out how many legs there were altogether on these 8 dinosaurs. You could write a problem like this:

$4 + 4 + 4 + 4 + 4 + 4 + 4 + 4 = 32$

This is a bit long though. You could think of multiplying 4 legs by 8 instead. You can write this as:

$4 \times 8 = 32$

You can only use multiplication when there are the same number of things in each group. You couldn't write a multiplication problem about the number of legs on two dinosaurs and a pterodactyl for instance, because the dinosaurs have 4 legs, but the pterodactyl really only has 2. You would have to write an addition problem like this:

$4 + 4 + 2 = 10$

There are two questions below. One can be answered by writing an addition problem and the other by writing a multiplication problem. Write either + or × after the questions below to show which is which.

If there are 9 cups and 3 have 1 straw, 3 have 2 straws and 3 have 3 straws, how many straws are there altogether? **[+]**

If there are 7 children coming and they each want 4 cakes, how many cakes must be baked? **[×]**

### Multiplying and dividing

In this book you will find division problems as well as multiplication problems. Division and multiplication are very closely linked. If you want to divide 28 by 7 it helps if you know that 7 multiplied by 4 is 28.

Division problems are about sharing amounts into equal groups. If 4 children had 12 rock cakes to share between them, they would each get 3 cakes. The problem for this would be:

$12 \div 4 = 3$

You can find the answers to all the puzzles in this book on pages 28 to 32.

Can you figure out whether you would use a multiplication problem or a division problem to answer the questions below? Write either × or ÷ in the boxes.

If there are 5 rows of stones in a wall and 15 stones in each row, how many stones are there altogether? **[×]**

Can you draw a ring around the multiplication problem that helps you solve the division problem?

$20 \div 4 =$

$2 \times 4 = 8$
or
$3 \times 4 = 12$
or
$\boxed{4 \times 5 = 20}$

Try not to use a calculator for any of the puzzles in this book.

This mammoth eats the same amount of food each day. If he eats 112 pounds in a week how much does he eat each day? **[÷]**

## Page 5

Name: Mr Og
18, 24, 30,
36, 42 48
54 60

Name: Mrs Og
9, 12, 15,
18, 21 24
27 30

Name: Grandma
6, 8, 10,
12, 14 16
18 20

Can you figure out which stone belongs to which member of the Og family? Put the correct name at the top of each stone and then write the next three numbers in each sequence.

Name: Grandpa
25, 30, 35,
40, 45 50
55 60

Name: Mog
30, 40, 50,
60, 70 80
90 100

Name: Zog
8, 12, 16,
20, 24 28
32 36

## Pages 6 and 7

### The market

Mrs. Og is at the market. Two of the traders are arguing about a box of apples. They want to know how many apples there are in the box. One man says that the problem is 4 × 6. The other man says it is 6 × 4.

Mrs. Og explains that they are both right. One man is counting the rows across and multiplying them by the number of columns. The other man is counting the columns and then multiplying them by the number of rows.

The important thing is that it doesn't matter, because 4 × 6 and 6 × 4 both give the answer 24.

Fruit and Vegetables

Can you write two problems for each of the boxes of fruit below?

$6 \times 5 = 30$
$5 \times 6 = 30$

$8 \times 6 = 48$
$6 \times 8 = 48$

$3 \times 4 = 12$
$4 \times 3 = 12$

The people of Ogtown use pebbles as money.

One of the traders has decided to make himself a chart to help him figure out the cost of his customers' shopping.

When he filled in the cost of 3 items at 7 pebbles per item, he drew his finger across from 3 until he got to the square that was underneath 7. He knew that 3 × 7 was 21, so he wrote 21 in that square.

Can you fill in the rest of the missing numbers for him?

An item is anything that the trader sells, like an orange or a pineapple or a banana.

You will only actually need to figure out the problems in the shaded area. The rest, like the problems on the opposite page, use the same numbers in a different order.

If you need to, you can use this chart to help you do some of the other problems in the book.

#### Cost per item in pebbles

| Number of items | 1 | 2 | 3 | 4 | 5 | 6 | 7 | 8 | 9 | 10 |
|---|---|---|---|---|---|---|---|---|---|---|
| 1 | 1 | 2 | 3 | 4 | 5 | 6 | 7 | 8 | 9 | 10 |
| 2 | 2 | 4 | 6 | 8 | 10 | 12 | 14 | 16 | 18 | 20 |
| 3 | 3 | 6 | 9 | 12 | 15 | 18 | 21 | 24 | 27 | 30 |
| 4 | 4 | 8 | 12 | 16 | 20 | 24 | 28 | 32 | 36 | 40 |
| 5 | 5 | 10 | 15 | 20 | 25 | 30 | 35 | 40 | 45 | 50 |
| 6 | 6 | 12 | 18 | 24 | 30 | 36 | 42 | 48 | 54 | 60 |
| 7 | 7 | 14 | 21 | 28 | 35 | 42 | 49 | 56 | 63 | 70 |
| 8 | 8 | 16 | 24 | 32 | 40 | 48 | 56 | 64 | 72 | 80 |
| 9 | 9 | 18 | 27 | 36 | 45 | 54 | 63 | 72 | 81 | 90 |
| 10 | 10 | 20 | 30 | 40 | 50 | 60 | 70 | 80 | 90 | 100 |

# Pages 8 and 9

**Perilous Pond**

Stepping stones numbers: 47, 14, 29, 42, 24, 37, 36, 40, 25, 44, 34, 54, 56, 27, 16, 12, 72, 9, 30, 64, 53, 49, 13, 59

Stone key:

| | | |
|---|---|---|
| $3 \times 4 = 12$ | $8 \times 2 = 16$ | $5 \times 5 = 25$ |
| $6 \times 4 = 24$ | $7 \times 6 = 42$ | $8 \times 5 = 40$ |
| $3 \times 9 = 27$ | $7 \times 8 = 56$ | $9 \times 6 = 54$ |

Grandpa Og and Zog have been playing with their discus near Perilous Pond. Unfortunately Grandpa threw the discus into the pond.

There are lots of stepping stones in Perilous Pond but not all of them are safe. If Grandpa or Zog step on a wobbly one they will fall in. This would be disastrous, because there are fierce, hungry, prehistoric fish in the pond, waiting to eat them.

Near the pond is a block of stone. It provides a key to which stones are safe. Can you help Zog and Grandpa to find a safe route to their discus? You need to figure out the answers to the problems and draw a ring around the numbers on the safe stones.

# Pages 10 and 11

**The circus**

The Ogs are at the circus, watching the jugglers. The juggler in blue has the number 8 on his suit. He is juggling with four balls which show the numbers 1, 2, 4 and 8. These numbers are called the factors of 8.

Can you figure out the factors of the other numbers on the jugglers' suits and write them on the balls? Each juggler is juggling with the correct number of balls.

The factors of a number are all the numbers that can be multiplied by another number to give you that number.

The factors of 8 are 1, 2, 4 and 8, because you can make 8 by multiplying 1 by 8, 2 by 4, 4 by 2 and 8 by 1.

Common factors are numbers that appear in more than one factor list.

The factors of 4 are 1, 2 and 4. The factors of 6 are 1, 2, 3 and 6. So, 1 and 2 are common factors of 4 and 6.

See if you can help Mog and Zog find the common factors of these pairs of numbers.

10 and 8 [1] [2]
18 and 12 [1] [2] [3] [6]
8 and 20 [1] [2] [4]
10 and 15 [1] [5]

Can you write the factors of each seat number on the back of the seat?

Seat numbers:
1 — 1
2 — 1,2
3 — 1,3
4 — 1,2,4
5 — 1,5
6 — 1,2,3,6
7 — 1,7
8 — 1,2,4,8
9 — 1,3,9
10 — 1,2,5,10
11 — 1,11
12 — 1,2,3,4,6,12
13 — 1,13
14 — 1,2,7,14
15 — 1,3,5,15
16 — 1,2,4,8,16
17 — 1,17
18 — 1,2,3,6,9,18
19 — 1,19
20 — 1,2,4,5,10,20

# Answers

## Pages 12 and 13

### The secret code

Mog and Zog are pretending to be spies. Mog has written a message to Zog, using their secret code. Below you can see what the message looks like.

| 78 | 64 | 72 | 87 | 72 | | 42 | 86 |
|---|---|---|---|---|---|---|---|
| T | H | E | R | E | | I | S |

| 42 | 80 | 96 | 42 | 86 | 42 | 85 | 84 | 72 | | 42 | 80 | 48 |
|---|---|---|---|---|---|---|---|---|---|---|---|---|
| I | N | V | I | S | I | B | L | E | | I | N | K |

| 42 | 80 | | 78 | 64 | 72 | | 99 | 42 | 80 | 48 | | 85 | 90 | 78 | 78 | 84 | 72 |
|---|---|---|---|---|---|---|---|---|---|---|---|---|---|---|---|---|---|
| I | N | | T | H | E | | P | I | N | K | | B | O | T | T | L | E |

To find out what Mog is telling Zog you have to crack the code.

Each letter of the alphabet is represented by a number. To find out what the number is you have to complete the multiplication problems. Zog has already figured out what A is, can you help him with the rest?

*Always multiply the units first.*

Zog is asking Mog a question in code. Can you figure out what it is?

| 56 | 64 | 72 | 87 | 72 | | 42 | 86 |
|---|---|---|---|---|---|---|---|
| W | H | E | R | E | | I | S |

| 93 | 75 | | 88 | 92 | 99 |
|---|---|---|---|---|---|
| M | Y | | C | A | P |

Can you write the answer in code too?

| 90 | 80 | | 78 | 64 | 72 | | 78 | 92 | 85 | 84 | 72 |
|---|---|---|---|---|---|---|---|---|---|---|---|

| A | B | C | D | | E | F | G | H | I |
|---|---|---|---|---|---|---|---|---|---|
| 23 | 17 | 44 | 14 | | 36 | 13 | 18 | 16 | 14 |
| ×4 | ×5 | ×2 | ×7 | | ×2 | ×7 | ×3 | ×4 | ×3 |
| 92 | 85 | 88 | 98 | | 72 | 91 | 54 | 64 | 42 |

*If you have any tens to carry over, write them under the bottom line of the problem. Don't forget to add them on, after you have multiplied the tens.*

| J | K | L | M | | N | O | P | Q | R |
|---|---|---|---|---|---|---|---|---|---|
| 15 | 16 | 14 | 31 | | 20 | 15 | 11 | 13 | 29 |
| ×4 | ×3 | ×6 | ×3 | | ×4 | ×6 | ×9 | ×5 | ×3 |
| 60 | 48 | 84 | 93 | | 80 | 90 | 99 | 65 | 87 |

| S | T | U | V | W | X | Y | Z |
|---|---|---|---|---|---|---|---|
| 43 | 13 | 15 | 12 | 14 | 19 | 15 | 17 |
| ×2 | ×6 | ×5 | ×8 | ×4 | ×5 | ×5 | ×3 |
| 86 | 78 | 75 | 96 | 56 | 95 | 75 | 51 |

12

13

## Pages 14 and 15

### The Ogtown picnic

Every year the people of Ogtown get together for an enormous town picnic. This year the Ogs have volunteered to do the shopping. They don't know exactly how many people will be coming, but they have estimated that they will need to cater for 1000 adults, 100 children and 10 dogs.

Can you calculate how many of each item they will have to buy and fill in the shopping list?

**Ogtown Picnic Shopping List**

| | |
|---|---|
| 20 | bones |
| 200 | cans of drink |
| 300 | little cakes |
| 2000 | buns |
| 400 | hot dogs |
| 40 | chocolate drops |
| 100 | packs of peanuts |
| 8000 | strawberries |
| 4000 | sandwiches |
| 80 | cans of dog food |
| 1000 | slices of cake |
| 3000 | cartons of mango juice |
| 500 | ice creams |

2 drinks per child
3 little cakes per child
4 sandwiches per adult
1 pack of peanuts per child
4 hot dogs per child
8 cans of dog food per dog
4 chocolate drops per dog
5 ice creams per child
3 cartons of mango juice per adult
1 slice of cake per adult
2 bones per dog
8 strawberries per adult
2 buns per adult

14

15

## Pages 16 and 17

### At the beach

Mog and Zog are spending the day on the beach with their friends, Mig and Tig Ig. They are building sandcastles. They have collected lots of shells, pebbles and pieces of seaweed to decorate them. They want to share the shells, pebbles and seaweed equally between them.

Count the number of shells. Can you figure out how many each child will get?

Decorate each castle with the correct number of shells.

Can you do the same with the pebbles and the seaweed?

The fishermen want to divide their catch equally between them. Can you help them by counting up the number of fish in the basket and then drawing the correct number of fish on the trays next to the fishermen?

All the fishermen should have an equal number of fish.

16

## Pages 18 and 19

### Off to Igville

Mr. Og is an avid walker and Mrs. Og sometimes likes to join him for a day out walking in the hills around Ogtown.

Today they are going to walk from Ogtown to Igville. Mr. Og wants to go one way, but Mrs. Og wants to go another way. They decide to go different ways and see who gets there first.

### How to play

To find out who arrives first, put a counter or coin on Mr. Og's starting point and one on Mrs. Og's. Look at the problem on Mr. Og's space and figure out the answer. There should be a remainder. Move forward the same number of spaces as the remainder. Do the same with the problem on Mrs. Og's space. Now go back to the space where Mr. Og's counter is and do that problem. Continue taking it in turns to do a problem on each path. Who gets there first? **Mrs. Og**

When you divide a number by another number it does not always divide equally. Sometimes there is a number left over. That number is called a remainder

In the problem 14 ÷ 3, 3 will go into 14 more than 4 times, but not as much as 5 times. So the answer is 4 remainder 2, because 4 threes are 12 and the difference between 12 and 14 is 2.

(r. means remainder)

39÷7
5 r. 4

23÷3
7 r. 2

24÷5
4 r. 4

48÷9
5 r. 3

41÷6
6 r. 5

33÷5
6 r. 3

You won't need to do all the problems on the path

37÷7
5 r. 2

32÷7
4 r. 4

41÷10
4 r. 1

IGVILLE

7÷4
1 r. 3

23÷4
5 r. 3

10÷3
3 r. 1

39÷9
4 r. 3

18÷8
2 r. 2

78÷10
7 r. 8

19÷2
9 r. 1

56÷9
6 r. 2

13÷3
4 r. 1

63÷8
7 r. 7

25÷6
4 r. 1

31÷7
4 r. 3

45÷8
5 r. 5

44÷5
8 r. 4

75÷9
8 r. 3

18

19

# Answers

## Pages 21

Not all of this shopping is for the Og family. Grandma and Grandpa have an elderly friend called Mrs. Ug. She finds walking difficult and so Grandma and Grandpa do her shopping for her.

Here is Mrs Ug's shopping list. Can you figure out how much she owes Grandma and Grandpa?

| Mrs. Ug's shopping | Pebbles |
|---|---|
| 3 bottles of milk | |
| 4 carrots | 48 |
| 2 cakes | 16 |
| 1 box of cereal | 70 |
| 2 blocks of cheese | 32 |
| 3 sausages | 48 |
| 2 yogurts | 27 |
| 1 pizza | 16 |
| 4 apples | 63 |
| 2 loaves of bread | 20 |
| 1 box of butter | 50 |
| 3 bananas | 22 |
| | 18 |
| TOTAL | 430 |

## Pages 24 and 25

### Mrs. Ig's flower shop

Grandma Og sometimes helps Mrs. Ig in her flower shop. Today she is looking at different ways of dividing the flowers into bunches.

At the bottom of the page you can see the lists Grandma has written. She is not very good at division problems and has made one mistake in each list. Can you find that mistake and draw a ring around it?

There is an easy way to check division problems. Multiply the answer by the number you divided by.

If the number you get is the same as the number you first started with the answer is right. If not, it is wrong.

Mrs. Ig is checking yesterday's takings. There were 411 pebbles in the cash register and she has a list of how many bunches of flowers she sold and what price they were.

| | pebbles |
|---|---|
| 6 bunches at 8 pebbles a bunch | 48 |
| 3 bunches at 13 pebbles a bunch | 39 |
| 8 bunches at 9 pebbles a bunch | 72 |
| 14 bunches at 6 pebbles a bunch | 84 |
| 4 bunches at 21 pebbles a bunch | 86 |
| 12 bunches at 7 pebbles a bunch | 84 |
| TOTAL | 413 |

When she has finished multiplying and adding up the answers, she ends up with a different number to the actual number of pebbles in the cash register.

Can you spot her mistake and draw a ring around it?

You can check a multiplication problem by dividing the answer by the number you multiplied by. The number you get should be the same as the first number in the multiplication problem.

**ROSES**
72 ÷ 12 = 6
6 bunches of 12 or
72 ÷ 4 = 18
18 bunches of 4 or
72 ÷ 6 = 13
3 bunches of 6 or
72 ÷ 3 = 24
24 bunches of 3

**TULIPS**
80 ÷ 4 = 20
20 bunches of 4 or
80 ÷ 8 = 10
10 bunches of 8 or
80 ÷ 5 = 15
15 bunches of 5 or
80 ÷ 20 = 4
4 bunches of 20

**CARNATIONS**
144 ÷ 18 = 8
8 bunches of 18 or
144 ÷ 9 = 16
16 bunches of 9 or
144 ÷ 6 = 24
24 bunches of 6 or
144 ÷ 4 = 35
35 bunches of 4

80 tulips

144 carnations

72 roses

## Page 23

Can you figure out the average scores for the rest of the team?

| Match | 1 | 2 | 3 | 4 | 5 | 6 | Average |
|---|---|---|---|---|---|---|---|
| Mrs Og | 46 | 30 | 42 | 38 | 20 | 46 | 37 |
| Zog | 58 | 24 | 67 | 14 | 5 | 48 | 36 |
| Mrs Ig | 21 | 47 | 38 | 26 | 11 | 55 | 33 |
| Mr Ig | 32 | 26 | 54 | 31 | 17 | 38 | 33 |
| Tig | 63 | 22 | 36 | 11 | 16 | 62 | 35 |

Grandma and Grandpa Og watch all the Pterodactyl's matches. Grandpa loves calculating averages. He doesn't just figure out each player's average number of runs, he figures out lots of other averages as well. Here are the figures he has written down in his notebook. Can you figure out all the averages?

| | Total number of Pterodactyl runs | Total number of opposition runs | Number of spectators | Number of sandwiches eaten |
|---|---|---|---|---|
| Match 1 | 243 | 180 | 62 | 36 |
| Match 2 | 195 | 240 | 73 | 24 |
| Match 3 | 250 | 182 | 54 | 34 |
| Match 4 | 176 | 165 | 88 | 38 |
| Match 5 | 108 | 295 | 65 | 43 |
| Match 6 | 312 | 234 | 120 | 29 |
| Average | 214 | 216 | 77 | 34 |

## Page 27

Sid is testing Mog to see how fast she can do her multiplication problems using his terrific tips.

Mog takes 3 minutes to do these problems. Can you beat Mog's time? When you have finished, check your answers and add on 10 seconds for every wrong answer.

Don't forget, you can change the order of the numbers in a multiplication problem and still get the same answer. So if you know a terrific tip for either of the numbers in the problem, use it.

3 × 5 = 15
10 × 6 = 60
9 × 4 = 36
8 × 11 = 88
9 × 9 = 81
3 × 10 = 30
11 × 9 = 99
5 × 5 = 25
8 × 6 = 48
3 × 9 = 27

9 × 10 = 90
5 × 8 = 40
9 × 2 = 18
11 × 6 = 66
2 × 5 = 10
5 × 7 = 35
9 × 8 = 72
6 × 9 = 54
10 × 7 = 70
4 × 5 = 20

Sid has made up a number puzzle for Zog. Can you help him fill it in?

| | | | | | | | |
|---|---|---|---|---|---|---|---|
| ¹3 | ²6 | | | ³2 | 0 | |
| | ⁴3 | 0 | | | 7 | |
| ⁵7 | | | | ⁶3 | 3 | |
| 7 | | ⁸4 | 5 | | 4 | 5 |
| | ⁹7 | 0 | | ¹⁰5 | 4 | |
| 2 | | | | 0 | | ¹¹1 |
| | ¹²2 | 0 | | ¹³2 | 0 | |

**Across**
1  6×6
3  5×4
4  6×5
6  3×11
7  9×5
8  5×9
9  7×10
10  9×6
12  10×2
13  2×11

**Down**
2  7×9
3  9×3
5  7×11
6  7×5
7  4×10
8  11×4
9  8×9
10  10×5
11  2×6